GW01418857

The Agnostic

The Agnostic

Mia Collins

Copyright © 2024 by Mia Collins.

Library of Congress Control Number: 2024905307
ISBN: Hardcover   978-1-6698-9074-4
                 Softcover   978-1-6698-9073-7
                 eBook   978-1-6698-9072-0

All rights reserved. No part of this book may be reproduced or transmitted in any form or by any means, electronic or mechanical, including photocopying, recording, or by any information storage and retrieval system, without permission in writing from the copyright owner.

This is a work of fiction. Names, characters, places and incidents either are the product of the author's imagination or are used fictitiously, and any resemblance to any actual persons, living or dead, events, or locales is entirely coincidental.

Any people depicted in stock imagery provided by Getty Images are models, and such images are being used for illustrative purposes only.
Certain stock imagery © Getty Images.

Print information available on the last page.

Rev. date: 03/12/2024

To order additional copies of this book, contact:
Xlibris
UK TFN: 0800 0148620 (Toll Free inside the UK)
UK Local: (02) 0369 56328 (+44 20 3695 6328 from outside the UK)
www.Xlibrispublishing.co.uk
Orders@Xlibrispublishing.co.uk
859134

CHAPTER ONE

Annnnnd...... "CUT!", that's a wrap. Don't bother with that scene just move on to the next ok,.... take a break. Everyone on set leaves their positions to talk to the other actors about the next scene, while Tabitha walks over to the bar and stands there. She's been feeling funny since she landed in Asheville, North Carolina, to take part in an American romantic comedy sports film about a minor league American baseball team. Jonny had taken her there as a surprise; he wanted to show her where he worked including what he did for a living. The problem was Tabitha wasn't feeling herself; she only had a small portion of plane food and also had only had a couple beers to drink on the way over yet she wasn't legally old enough. Johnny had said I can't buy you a beer but while I'm gone you can have a bit of mine 'if you like' just say you took it I didn't give it to you if anyone asks. Tabitha couldn't handle beers; she was too slim and most of all too young but that didn't stop her from trying new things because she trusted him. It made her feel grown up. She had a job after all so that's maturity as far as she was concerned. Arriving at the studio he threw her straight in the deep end "go and walk round the set act natural." __He said you're playing Jane, and you're seventeen ok, ok, she replied. __ yeah, fine with that she was used to acting older to get into bars with him anyway she was always hanging round with older groups so that's where it led to bars or parties.

As the scenes were being done she was really out of it to a point she didn't know where she was one min then her head would spin she'd be ok get back with it and then off again a burst of energy. She was having a blast. Jonny said look over there go walk round the bar it's kevan,[He was a major movie star] at that she was off like a shot, she had been a huge fan with an equally big crush on kevan. She walks round twice as he's sitting in a booth she looks over smiles and points as thats her thing she points when she flirts but being drunk she was wobbly, she said something this sparked kevan then his hand shot up waved '...cut, she's not meant to talk,' so she goes back then Johnny says go again, she does it again and again, in hindsight the first one was the best as she only got worse after that, it was the drink she was too wrecked by this point to work or play this part and it was Jonny's fault for allowing her to drink. [Tabitha was hammered.] What sorta impression is it to turn up to a massive hit movie with A cast stars and she's off her head.

Kevan approaches Tabitha and says hi 'I thought I better come and say hi, and you're a natural,' Tabitha's head was really spinning at this stage and she said something really embarrassing and wanted the ground to swallow her up immediately after speaking. "What makes you think I'm natural? I may be a blond" and that smiles at him flirtingly,[she knew she messed up,] he said "I'm married I can't be thinking that"__ and at that he said "are you with him?" Jonny'? She looks shocked, "NO, he's my friend' ', as she peers across the room to him as Jonny is running off out the door towards the cameras. "Where's he going"? He better not be leaving me. He always leaves me and I can't find my way home.

Genuinely concerned but he was watching it all from the cameras, all the mics were hidden in the sets very cleverly hidden. Jonny runs over to her telling her to go outside. __It's a fight scene, no she said I don't like fights, I'll stay here. The next scene was the dance floor. Timo came over [one of the three stars in the film], do you want to dance with me? ok, so she headed for the dance floor scene but she sat down, as he reached his hand out would you dance with me she smiles and looks bashful gets up and does a little spin under his arm, the music playing was 'born to be bad' what a great hit, she but suddenly felt dizzy so she sat down, so CUT again,[shouted] more girls came over and he danced with the lot while Tabitha sat by the fake door, which she'd tried to open twice looking for the loo.

At this point, Jean came over. He was a movie critic. His partner was in the bar booths too. They had a show to air so they did the journalism on many films, that means they get to be in the films and enjoy the perks. He sat next to Tabitha. If you're not going to dance then at least clap, "quick the cameras are coming over now be ready," oh i'm so not photogenic same he replied then you're in the wrong job resulting in him having a little laugh. He was kind and exceedingly helpful. She needed someone to sit rightfully to put her straight a majority of the time that day. At her age she needed complete guidance and wanted knowledge more than anything. The next scene after a brief getting ready for the next setting up cameras while gathering background cast into the bar booths basically like who's walking round or dancing on set in their place while Kevan went to his position in the booth. "Action ". This time Tabitha was sitting in a booth unfortunately she was totally spinning out from the alcohol by this point she could hardly see or react in any sensible compos-mentis form, she was talking too much, this angered Jonny as he hastily approached her and gave her a shoulders a good shake. He shouted at Tabitha shoving her into the seat firmly and said shut up and stop talking, at this point Jean came and sat across from her he was comforting and kind, he said drink, drink your beer, "she replied I'm not allowed to drink I don't drink," he said its a fake beer, oh yea, she thought silly girl, so holding back the tears running down her face from Jonny making her cry she had the silliest expression in that scene as she looks traumatized despite the fact that she was just emotional. Now fighting two emotions at the same time as Suzan, one of the major stars turns around and says "Will you stop out staging me hunny" giving her a big cuddle, making her laugh again but the make up was already running down her face. hrs__Prior to this, Jonny had put her to bed on the plane as it was a long flight, she felt he was doing her hair and also make-up but was too tired to stay awake or care so let him get on with it, he wanted her ready as soon as they exited the plane. [He made her feel like a doll the way he treated her to be honest if there was an expression to explain it.]

Back at the bar scene her tears were flowing, Jean had sat down opposite to Tabitha he explained his job and why he was there, he was the only person apart from Suzan who had the patients to deal with her being all over the place.

There was a highly embarrassing moment for her that day, as it happens It was super embarrassing in a way as she went hours without finding a loo, following that same day she passed out for a few moments and wet herself. In a flash she was awoken by Jonny having run over to her thrown a fake beer while he was shaking her shaking it up all down her top and legs as she jumped up awake with the cold shock, he whispered "I'm saving you I'm saving you!" as he thought fast and made it look like she was covered in beer. She was so deep asleep she hadn't realized she had wet herself in hindsight, so she went with it and said Jonny you idiot i'm soaked. Leaving a big puddle on the seat and floor. Others ripped into her for this but Jonny put them in their place chastising them.

Next scene; let's get ready everybody, the director Ron shouts. One of the actresses grabs Tabitha's arm and takes her into a cupboard to change, she gives her a new pair of dry jeans but the top stays to be tucked in this time. Jonny runs over and gives her a cowgirl hat with hair attached; he said it's to look different in the next scene. So they begin filming, Tabitha was supposed to walk behind Susan to the ball game, but she kept grabbing her even in the bar scenes she was practically swinging off her neck so drunk just having too much fun and Suzan was like "I can't work like this!" as she laughed it off, trying to do the scene again. Tabitha kept saying "you just said that" but in Suzans accent which was a lovely southern American one, so Tabitha kept trying to attempt it but it became more annoying than funny, she didn't know when to stop but Suzan took it on the chin and was patient more than she needed to be.

They even talked about how Suzan met her new lover on that set which was so sweet as Tabitha had just said 'I think you should date him.' 'Suzan said that's so funny you saying that I went out with him last week.' As tabitha was jumping around so much, she would sit funny on a chair, one leg up knee tucked under her elbow so to speak, it was just comfortable when the other actress who lent her the jeans had asked can she use that sitting position it's great, of course you can you don't have to ask me so at that was that the scene was done the way Tabith used to usually sit. But then she had to sit properly after that.

___ Suzan is repeatedly trying to do her walking to the ball game scenes Tabitha is too much hanging off her arm. She laughs it off before another actress takes Tabitha ahead by the arm, and the filming commences. "Come on we need to stand out, let's skip," nobody else is skipping and so they were laughing all the way to the ball game. On arrival there it wasn't really the scene for the game yet and everyone would walk back to the bar again for more shoots. The loos were all props and nobody would guide her to any real loos so while at the ball game she peed in a fake loo, the actress laughed and said there's no water in them fake loo's, but there is now and cracks up. Jonny walks her round some other outdoor scenes while he pretends to be her boyfriend, in one scene they had a little row and got told off [deleted scenes would be an interesting watch]. Jonny included was intoxicated by this point, he was wrong in bringing her over in that state that resulted in her getting in trouble for it too.

So the day went on it was great fun Jonny had to keep his head low as he wasn't in that film. At the end he brang over an image release form for her to sign, she was reluctant but he convinced her to fill it in explaining __ "you trust me right I want the best for you." He took her hand and guided her round introduced her to the partner of Jean another journalist his name was Roger, of course Tabitha burst out laughing thought Jonny was kidding and being rude, thinking it was some Roger him joke which another epic fail on her behalf of making a awful first impression but he laughed too which was just luck or him being polite. He would've known what Jonny was like anyway and took him with a pinch of salt and smiled it off. Tabitha shook his hand and said hello. Jonny pipes up and says be nice to this man he's the one doing your write up. Don't scare me she thought like that as she peers across at Jonny.

There was a scene outside with them hitting the balls in the cages for practice swings, Johnny's her fake boyfriend walking along behind the cages he says don't speak, _ "why can't I speak?" As she pipes up and that's it "CUT"! There were more cut scenes that day because Tabitha was talking when she shouldn't be.. Oops! Susan had sat her down at the very end and discussed where Tabitha was in her life at that time and she had just left school so it was a chat about her exams and how she wasn't sure how she would go in life, some were A's some were rubbish but a majority of good results to get by but she wasn't happy she wanted more knowledge she always felt she needed more wanted to know so much more, talking to older experienced people to her was like she became a little sponge therefore she hoped to soak it all up and learn from them all. [That being her biggest desire was later taken from her as the brain injury inflicted destroyed her future.]

As many years went by now in her thirties, she bumped into Jonny in a bar one afternoon, he was furious upon seeing her at first then he suddenly shouts you're that famous girl you're Tabitha who was in the baseball movie with Kevan, Suzan, and Timo. He spouts off the journalists names too but Tabitha wasn't understanding him. This was a time her memory was gone during the twenty six years of bliss and not recalling her life, her life stories all wiped. He tried desperately so hard to make her recollect, but this just confused her even more. Then he suddenly in a split second waved his hands as in sorry and suddenly piped up with "do you wanna jam,?" he pulled up a drum and the other older guy grabs a guitar. He was trying to get her to sing, "come on Tabitha sing," he was playing a song she didn't even know, "no I can't sing", he had a horrified look on his face, suddenly his mood swung instantaneously, became very angry jumping up from his seat threw the drum and ran out the bar. The man on the guitar was like "don't worry he's only upset because you can't remember him." that didn't ring any bells with her she was standing there mystified.

That interaction didn't reciprocate; his actions were just odd so she left the bar to go meet others she arranged to meet that afternoon. Not realizing that in forthcoming years she would ever begin to regain her life back or knowing the dragon's tail end of her story would be the beginning of a movie, and one of her missing memories were her being even as background being in a 'Box Office movie.'

As the corrugation of life unfolds she's come to the conclusion even with all the bad the good really did outweigh it after all.

During that time she was beginning to learn to deal with the flashbacks and was able to sit and laugh to herself about her life. There were a lot of funny moments to remember she wanted to hold onto, as she reached out to tell people about her incredible past she had nothing but hostility towards for speaking out. Why can't she speak out? It's her life and if she wants to tell her story it's her right to leave behind a legacy of how life was in those years in this world. It seemed to bother people when she talked about the happy memories more than the sad, what's that about why do people like the doom and gloom and can't just be happy for someone it's quite a baffle. But not everyone wants to see you happy and it's a good opportunity to wean into new circles with friends who support you and not keep you down so you can't thrive and plan for a better future. Not only that there were moments of dark times too and secrets she remembered Jonny made her keep and promise to never tell on him. He did something terrible once to her, life changing that would affect her from then on, but the flight abroad was his attempt to make it up in his own odd way. There was a time his words were; I feel responsible and I'd like to help you. But she soon put it behind her and cracked on with her life, without him around so much she wasn't able to look back even if she wanted to; it was no longer there; he no longer existed in her world, but she had no power over this fact.

After the shooting of the scenes in America.__During the flight back they had to rush to catch the plane to England Johny had switched into a furious mood, after Tabitha wet herself from not being allowed to go to the loo but once from leaving England and once in the states in the day it was bound to happen she burst her banks, she would laugh about this in years to come. Johnny shoved her into a first class cabin with a sliding door, she didn't know how to fold the chair down into a bed so paced and sat, eventually she nodded off in the chair. She was told to stay inside by the air hostess firmly as Jonny said to her "you know that thing we talked about on the way over here can we go have some fun if you like?" She told Tabitha to not come out, half hr later she could hear them in the cabin next door banging away during the hostess break, Johnny used women for sex it was something Tabitha had seen many times often he'd have two or three in one evening if she had a pound for catching him shagging someone round the back of a club or in a closet she'd be rich. He had a sex addiction and he didn't care much about who he used and what they looked like as long as they were female. He had one of every allsort if you can put it that way every size, every colour, every age. Tabitha didn't really take much notice of him she was used to him at this point so laughed them off, she tried to give him advice explaining to him to stay loyal to his girlfriend but he never listened it was who he was he clearly didn't really know what real love was she didn't think if he did he'd of stayed loyal to them. If that's what he wanted to do it's down to him, he was definitely mentally ill in some form but she didn't know what his label was. He was only really being a danger to himself risking his health.

After the plane landed they walked out and straight into a car he had waiting. The man who drove them home to Jonny's house wasn't even legally old enough to drive. He had no license, Jonny had said "well done man see you can drive you did it" handed him the cash for collecting us. As Jonny ran round the back of his manor house to collect his car from the car port, the man who was driving them was supposed to leave but suddenly fiercely like the act of mentally ill [stemming toward a psychopath] person just punched Tabitha the ground saying "if it was me taking you home I'd teach you a lesson." She was a fifteen/sixteen year old girl so exactly what sorta lesson did he mean? Why did she need a lesson teaching for what being laced with booze while underage was not taken care of properly and wetting herself because she hadn't had experience in drinking ? Why was he so evil? It was later

on that she realized in the period of memories coming
to surface that in hindsight she suddenly knew that this
man who drove them home from the airport was also
that fat screaming cry baby kid who used to ruin bingo
every friday nt in the village hall. His dad was the caller
and he organized it for the village to bring something to
the place less dull. This kid used to scream, play up have
tantrums beat his sister up who was half his size regularly,
the mother seem to be the one who was always trying to
protect the little girl from him and the father giving him
a clout round the side of his head now and then bring him
into line. One night the caller announced he wasn't doing
it anymore consequently bingo was going to stop. To the
solemn mood change in the room as he explained he was
dying from cancer. The chubby brat piped up and cried
bursting into tears and violently threatened everyone who
was looking at him making a holy show of himself. He
said if my dad dies, I'll kill my mum and sister. I hate
them, and he meant every word. This boy had serious
issues. [Probably would have been best if it was him who
died in place as he grew up to be one of the most sinister
monsters of all time.] __hindsight is a wonderful thing!

Some years in between Jonny had picked Tabitha up one evening he said we're going to a party, come on hop in the car, they went to a town nearby first of all to collect one other man, Tabitha knew him from the bar she worked in. Shortly after they arrived at this farm house in the village her and Jonny lived, it was alone in a field, a rural spot for a home although upon entering it felt neglected and cold she would describe it as poverty stricken perhaps just lack of interest or care. It was the chubby brats birthday she was never able fully or have knowledge as his real age was never disclosed, it was ten minutes they stayed there for before the ugly ogre had his mother in a choke hold he was strangling her and pressed his knuckles into her skull showing off there was clearly some mental illness in him nobody wanted to face. The mother burst into tears. She spent the day cleaning the house putting up balloons for him all day and he didn't appreciate it; he just wanted to hurt and humiliate his mum.

The father dying wasn't the cause. He clearly was already an awful lad in the making while he was alive but as he grew so big his strength on an evil man wasn't an ideal combination.

He ended up being one of Jonny's doormen and background bodyguards for his nights out on the town lurking in the background like a vulgar cretin who didn't fit anywhere in society this spoke volumes of Jonny having him around though but no worse than Tabitha having Bia both of them had a evil jealous person intertwined in their lives under there noses and neither of them saw it, was it planned as the two ogres were incredibly close too.

Was Jonny aware of how perverted his doorman was all along the fact he kept hiring him years after he was in prison for raping dogs means he turned a blind eye to that crime. His real age was misled in the paper with a historical photo as he was twice as big and older looking in real life than the photo the papers had used. Jonny had power in the papers working along with providing news to them regularly and setting up consequently sending in their own photos to look like the press caught them but Tabitha was often there and see it was his mates taking the photos as the exact spot and back ground she started to work out how the media really works. It's not all what you'd expect. But she understood the reason they tell the world they live in one place and reside in another or they're here or there is to protect them which is understandable, so by time you see the news it's quite old. But the setting up of it is like reading a big fat lie when you know the truth. But she respected it as everyone had a right to privacy and safety no matter what so she kept hush.

___ To the jist of the story the brat at bingo grew up to be one of the worst perverts that you'd not want loose on the streets, so why Jonny had taken him under his wing was no hope in him helping or changing him now. Jonny would see the best in someone and he had this idea he can help them out of a rum place a dark place in their harrowing lives, but he didn't spend enough time focusing on them for long enough he had too many irons in the fire hence things went on under his nose unnoticed this could bring him down with the ship if this information had been exposed.

There was a lot of propaganda going on in the news as Tabitha knew that the person fighting Jonny was holding back from telling the truth. It's none of her business not her problem but she felt like the other person deserved the truth to be told to them but she decided no, keep out of it now too many peoples lives at stake innocent lives many many of them used and discarded, not their fault they didn't need to be involved in it all but they deserve so much more than they have. Tabitha knew all of Jonny's secrets but she chose to keep it zipped. She felt like the right thing to do is nothing in this case. What has she got to gain by destroying someone else's lives, nothing, and she's had no hostility towards him as he has done so much good for her and given her all her good memories which she hoped now would stay but that's not clear at this point. But the memories were beginning to fade again.

It was becoming apparent to Tabitha when she thought it was over and the flashbacks had stopped she recalled it all there would be more trickling in still. Five years of a twenty six year memory loss coming back faster and clearer than ever. She had a gold mine in her hands at this point but decided she'd still be the girl who she always was, the one who stuck up for her friends and not bring them down holding a power over someone isn't who she is. She had to process more, this stranger at her door who was the sick criminal who hurt the kids was the weird fat kid at bingo. How did she not notice or ever see this man?

Perhaps she only seen him when she had been spiked, which would explain it, he had told her during one of the attacks that he was from the same area as her and said the house address too, she had no idea what he was on about but in between punches she wasn't interested in his life story. But suddenly she had identified him properly and was able to tell the police more about who he was and how he lurked and who he mixed with. This wasn't going to be a smear campaign she had to expose this vile man without doing harm to Jonny's reputation too. She knew if Jonny knew what he had done to the children and how many others he probably harmed over the years Jonny would have wiped his hands and sacked him from his team. One thing Jonny loves is kids and he'd protect them, even if he wasn't the greatest to have around at times with his drink and drugs, he wouldn't harm them.

When they were first starting out all those years ago before they had kids, he had got himself banned from visiting Tabitha when she was a young girl. He would be chased out by her granddad a few times fist in air or a stick raised to him and chased out the gate. "Get out get out never come back I don't want to see the likes of ye here again and stay away from her." Her grandparents believed he was a bad influence; his own grandmother had told her nan she was ashamed of the way he behaved at times with girls. He would grow up eventually nevertheless. Tabitha didn't fully believe that Jonny would ever be capable or be able to choose just one person or one thing he could stick to for very long before he was bored and go onto the next shortly after or even the same day. The only person he was hurting in the long run was himself after all.

There were equally two sides to any one. What is good and what is bad usually has a balancing point; he didn't spend a lot of time in the middle of that scale. But she still found him funny and would rather laugh when she looked back at the hilarious times they had over the years and try to hold onto the good memories.

CHAPTER TWO

Prison

Back in the present time swifty[the brat] had landed himself in prison for drug dealing on a large level. Rumor had it he had a sting consequently he was set up by some of the enemies he had gathered many over the years from bragging about his sick fetishes, earning money harming children, women, men, and even dogs, he had no ability to feel empathy or love let's face it he bragged when he had a few beers he opened up like a truth serum was popped in his drink. He was just a psychopath, simple as that but not a very bright one. Now he was inside he was easy to get to. His enemies had him right where they wanted him. This is now the time who was going to do it, how and when, there was a queue of people lined up who wanted to take the name of the hero who took out the sexual predator. He had already got into scuffs in prison he loved a fight but now the tables were turned he certainly didn't have his drugs to put them to sleep before he could fight in an unfair advantage, but now he had to be a man and fight them all sober, fair and square but he wasn't used to men standing up to him his usual was weak children he would beat up, rape and break their bones with nothing but a smile on his face and nothing between the ears for any thought or regrets, he needed to be eliminated.

The morning came, as the prison bells ring to let everyone know their doors were unlocked, at this point they could all head out make their way down to the canteen, in line heading down the stairs from his cell, he made his way down the steps, his eyes were in the back of his head paranoid clearly as all onlookers by this point all rants were on him. Everybody by the second week inside knew what he was. Life was about to become incredibly uncomfortable for him.

___" *A vernal impulse from out of the blue from The Emerald Isle".*

Tabitha was heading home from a job one afternoon when she heard the phone ping, she had a msg come through from a IRA member, the number would be used which later to be destroyed there was no replying to these men, she knew how it worked, the family had always been pro IRA, not something to be proud of in a political way she wasn't into politics it was just part of the surroundings as she had grown up in a republican family. She wasn't allowed to mix with the English growing up. It caused a lot of problems and in fact socially destroyed a lot of her childhood, it also made a lot of problems go away too. The lads had heard what had happened she didn't tell them but someone had, she didn't intend to be involved in this it wasn't her style she wanted no part in any violence or wrongdoing, two wrongs don't make a right. But somehow they knew one of them in particular had a big soft spot for Tabitha and in addition he cared tremendously for her at one time in his life but she couldn't commit or stay in that world not then and not ever.

She wasn't about to tell him either, she had this msg saying "A little bird told me something, you should have come to me. I'm not happy by far, but mark my words, it'll be sorted. "Up the Ra"~ as fast as she could read it it was gone. Oh no, what the hell have you done who told them? That's the last thing she needs now, did they know who he was and where he was, the less she knew the better, in fact she wished he hadn't msg her, but his anger towards her to not letting him know about her children being hurt had pushed him over the edge, he was a mean Irish fella who wasn't to be reckoned with at the best of times, but one thing in him that was gold was he never laid an hand on a woman or children he was ideal In a sense hmm. (irish gentleman.)

Evening had come but Tabitha was wide awake half the night worried why she had to know at all, it felt like her grandparents had reached out from the grave in a fury as if they were alive they'd of reached to the Ra for help right while the iron was hot. He wouldn't have had the chance to strike again and nor were the others by this stage safe from the wrath of the irish who were well known by taking war into their own hands.

Over a period of many years every time the news was on she was half expecting to see one of them on it.. The anticipation was grueling but she knew it was only a matter of time,….they didn't wait for karma the Ra sorted it themselves.

Enough time had gone by life was pretty good by this point, work was good, friends she had made and life wisdom had helped her to keep away from certain characters, her life was either up there in the stars taking part in a big screen movie or down as low as being attacked one extreme to the other, but other than that she was extremely happy with life, things could be better money wise that's everyone these days mind, but making the most of what you have while you have a short time left on this earth is to enjoy every minute of it and that she did. She was an extreme optimist always looking on the bright side and she was now counting her blessings.

___In the prison there was certain roles, jobs and responsibilities that everyone had, and this cretin of a human being who by now was known by all and was constantly under the protection of the screws they didn't want to protect him it was just their job and paperwork would get messy if they turned their backs it can come back onto their job. Eyes were on Swifty whether he was aware they knew what he was is unknown but some of the rants may have been obvious and he would be keeping his head low. His job was to mop the floors he lacked intelligence so cooking wouldn't be his thing plus he'd probably eat it all being such a glutton.

Some visitors he had were secretly passing back the latest news which through mutual people they knew she would hear he was having a hard time, and had taken a few unpleasant confrontations. In other words he took a beating, there must have been a few outnumbering him as he was very like a neanderthal in size, big, clumsy and slow witted.

__Karma was knocking on his metaphorical door !

A friday night had come along the cell doors were still open and the men were allowed to mix until the bells would ring to get to their rooms for bed, and lock up time. But the period of sneaking contraband to one another was the highlight of their days inside be it fags or food which was Swifty's favourite thing. Was he aware of the men sneaking the food to him, the treats the chocolates he so loved were tampered with, was he about to be given a taste of his own medicine?

Tabitha had no idea what was going on, who, where, or when it could take place, days, months or years, one at a time, but one thing she did know they had a mark on their heads by this point.

Evening had arrived and the moon was rising, it was a beautiful red sky, a shepherd's delight as they say, and within the walls of prison everything was about to be as red as the sky.

The evenings were getting darker earlier on not that all had cells with windows with bars to see this glory but they knew it was some of them looked forward to seeing again when they dreamed of getting out. The lads who he had made pals with were the geeky tiny little men they were more into fraud than violence they had the mastermind he was the braun they must have seen he being big could be a good body guard for them while they do their dirty work.

[Even so everyone is about looking after themselves at the end of the day. Flash back; Swifty was bragging about Jonny's secret affairs and love childs laughing at how many he had people thought he was mad, he used to say; "Do you realize Jonny has thirty nine kids" and his wife don't even know… he has had four while he's been married to her, then laugh about it. He was quite odd to be honest the weird stuff he said during the attack made no sense at all to Tabitha, and how he would talk of Jonny behind his back was the ultimate low life. Why did Jonny mix with this sicko?]

Prison; __"Alright mate?" _another inmate who sounded like he was from london improbably towards Swifty tried to spark up a contraband exchange.

Did you get the dollar for the goods man? We got the stuff you wanted, "mars bars man I'll call you, you kinky bastard, we know what you want these for ya dirty fucker." ~ Swifty laughed it off but felt embarrassed but no shame although he hated being the center of everyone's joke. He knew he had to uphold a position he was inside for fairly long stretch being caught with the violent porn on his lap top and other things involving drugs the sorta drugs the normal addict doesn't need, date rape stuff included which had the screws keeping a closer eye on him because of that.

But then they forgot to watch his friends inside. The two men came into the cell and handed him the treats as it was too early for him he couldn't claim anything for eight weeks or earn enough money yet inside for his own clothes or fags or whatever he wanted, so he was reliant on contraband trade at this point and he was into men anyway so he would pay them in kind if need be he didn't shy away from anything.

As he began to indulge he was unaware they had drugged his food, they had added enough to tranquilize a horse. The intention was to slaughter him while he was unconscious but it had taken them so long to get to see him eat it as they had distracted him that by time it kicked in it was lock up time so they missed the chance by minutes to cut his throat. He slept like a baby and in the morning he didn't remember a thing. So he was none the wiser the attempt to kill him had even occurred he woke thinking he was just sick from the bugs going round covid perhaps, in the back of his mind he shifted perhaps they did spike him but nothing happened so he let his guard down and thought they liked him. They had got away with it by the skin of their noses, they had no idea what they were doing, they had no military training or street wise they were just fraudsters who know how to make money, so out of their league but a lucky close escape so far. They would now have to wait for the next delivery for the drugs to be brought in to try again.

Outside in the meantime the Ra were still planning on their ways of getting to him they didn't want some small time nobody's to do this it had to be done properly slowly and painfully as far as they were concerned if someone got to him first they'd be miffed to say the least. It takes a lot of planning to do this and has to be done by someone ideally who isn't getting out but they like to send in a man to give orders on how it's got to be done. It's not good enough to just be shot, drowned or stabbed, it has to be brutal, violent and painful.

These orders were given quietly during an opportunist visitor who would come in undercover as a girlfriend of an inmate. Someone who wouldn't spark suspicion.

They want the man to suffer and when they say they suffer it'll be counting every child he hurt in numbers and adding a few to that on top for each wound. He will die slowly with a thousand cuts consequently and fortunately for every one of his victims he won't be drugged like he did to them kids, besides if he was unlucky to wake he would wake with parts missing plus never be able to harm a child again. They would remove his manhood last were the orders. But he was now on the waste of space list including to be eliminated as soon as the opportunity arose. They do have more important things to do after all. But being English was another good reason as far as they are concerned. A republican family is hard to stop the generations along the way from following in their footsteps, the ones who leave and go live abroad have a better hope in severing the ties to that political truss. So he's not aware the Ra are gunning for him yet. There are other gangs inside who may get to him first, but they've tried to lay orders to the rest of the cartel to leave it, perhaps reword to request a deal with. It's their man like a treaty in other words, they weren't trying to make enemies here but wanted him to be their man. __He was their target!

Swifty's father would be ashamed of how he turned out and what he's done, he wouldn't of wanted him to keep on tormenting his sister and mother, unless behind closed doors his father was the same nobody knows but himself, along with to see how much he loved his dad by the way he cried for him nobody consoled him, Tabitha didn't see his mother give him a hug to console him when he had the shock of hearing his dad was going to die soon, and why announce it in front of the children that way in front of the entire village? That should be a family private matter.

Regardless he had that childhood trauma but his own behavior was beyond reasoning with he needed a special needs school to get him in line. There was no reconciling excuse to how or why he turned into the monster he was. He grew up hating women as well as being a real mental case similar to a lot of serial killers and rapists, but he was indistinguishable. There was no helping him at this stage; the best thing to do would be to put him down like a rabid dog. When you look back to his historical story and his past, to wonder what could have been done differently, what made him this way? How much abuse did he receive or was he born this way? Is his amygdala volume lower than a normal persons? It was clearly obvious he didn't have a perfectly formed brain, perhaps running eighteen percent less than others were, which was common in psychopaths therefore it was less functioning to cause some of his symptoms. ~ But who cares, he was a monster. ~

It's too late now to annalyse him?

__Come on lads what has to be done tonight, "let's get the bastard we got orders get it over with so we can get back to a good night's rest and chill until the next nonce piece of shit walks in and ruins our peace in here man…...."

Months later, they didn't give a toss about no sob childhood trauma he had he made a decision to plan and harm to rape kids and dogs, women and even men alongside teenage boys there was no limit. One of the drivers who worked for Jonny had just had a call from him, he was clearly distraught but the driver was laughing about one of his sons who died in an accident saying; "oh well he had loads more kids what's one loss, he never seen him for years anyway like why pretend he cares now too late." he didn't care he only wanted money and fame he was a jealous man.

He also had bragged how swifty 'his best mate' had drugged Jonny and had raped him when he was supposed to be helping him get home but the dark side of the story is there was images going round online he had took of himself raping Jonny. It was a vile accusation to make about him, he wasn't gay but his staff were really horrid behind his back, it comes down to jealousy. They were no oil paintings themselves.... In Fact real ugly men with vile bodies had a personality to match. Jonny's awful team who he believed to be his friends who were bragging about his private life left right and center. Little did he know half the stories in the paper were coming from men close to him in his team. Therefore it'll be no loss when one is out of the picture, it's a blessing he will never know how much he was stabbing him in the back all along trying to take his name down with him. Is there a justification to top someone when their friends don't know what he did?

The world says yes !

CHAPTER THREE

T he world went on after the news of his execution, nobody said a word, the news had got wind of his crimes and reasons why he was murdered but nobody was found guilty for some reason there was a blind spot in the prison where the cameras had gone down mysteriously the day before, the engineers weren't told on time to arrive or have time to fix them, what's the odds they all went down at once. The funeral was fairly quiet, his mother, his sister and her children didn't come along which seemed odd or perhaps they were grateful he was no longer their problem. The problem is when you commit a crime to such an extreme level you cannot expect empathy even his own mother probably sighed a deep breath of relief. Now he meets his father on the other side to feel his wrath and shame and his time if you believe that sorta thing it's now time to face his consequences. ~"The Agnostic".

Tabitha hadn't seen the news; it was several years later she had come to the knowledge of his demise. What was most alarming was she now knew he was serious about his promise which meant the others were still on his list to be next in line for he was coming for them now.

It wasn't going to look good for her if all these people were being knocked off however many years apart, she was trying to reach out to him no, more leave it now but it was too late he had made it clear it was now his war as he felt for her children like they were his own and adored them all. Nobody was walking away from this alive at this point. Tabitha didn't want to be intertwined with this.

The fear was setting in she felt like she had blood on her hands by this point, but it was too late now she had no power over what the Ra did and no knowledge it was them for all she knew one of the other gangs got hold of him and she was worrying about nothing right, let's think this through they're all targets inside at the end of the day. Her ability to just be happy really bothered some people ie; the ones now in line for their graves about to be dug..

All while she sleeps the rest of the world is jumping hoops around her world and for what ?

"~ for the children ! that's what, Wrath !~"

As each day passes she remembers additional missing memories, most of the time they were now by this point happy ones. The good outweighs the bad but that doesn't mean the bad will be brushed aside and not dealt with. It has to be faced full throttle.

Jonny had led her one day after asking her to meet him in town, he led her into a garage where an overweight sweaty man sat grinning. It was dark and smelly in there and Jonny was in a vile mood she had no idea why. He closed the shutters down as they entered like it was some secret. But she remembers the location.

So the man in the garage, what Tabitha had come to realize in later life, was swifty, but she didn't know who he was that day. He was a fugly stranger as far as she was concerned she didn't like the way he looked or spoke. He gave her the creeps. But that was surely him he worked in a garage fixing cars, he was younger in those days she years later realised he always lurking in the back ground all along with Jonny, why did Jonny mix with dog raping pervert? Something had changed in Jonny. The fat guy grabbed Tabitha by the throat while attacking her, Jonny came in shouting and pushed her out the door telling her to run off. He knew his friend was a predator, so why did he keep him as a friend surely he should of distanced himself from this man it was trying to bring Jonny's reputation down but Jonny didn't see it, he had a friend who was jealous of him but he didn't see it right under his nose.

This was the same fat man she used to see Bia sneaking off behind bar alleys with but she hadn't put two and two together at the time she just thought Bia was earning her money as she slept with men for money to pay for her drug addiction, she didn't realize he was her boyfriend. But it explains why Tabitha and Jonny both had been run down by these two undesirables. Swifty and Bia were a team of two, a pair of sickos who both suffered equal mental health issues from childhood abuse that led to their adult psychosis.

So years went by but she no longer remembered who he was in her future, due to the skull fracture hole in her head and brain damage. It seemed a lot to process, but the boy Jonny she grew up with was no longer there who he had become, he was a jackal and hyde at this point in his life. If he could get off the drugs perhaps he would go back to who he was before who knows, but it was no longer her problem he was no longer himself. Who has he become? In hindsight the two men both had mummy issues both abused by their mothers and somehow both grew up to be perverts of a different form. Although she felt Jonny only had a sex addiction, the other guy wasn't even human.

During one of the attacks Swifty was spouting all kinds of stories he made no sense to her at the time, as she had no memory of who Jonny was then, but she remembers him saying something about a man called Jonny his boss, who had thirty nine kids and how he abused women and used them as incubators, he would be obsessed with making babies and mass breeding, she figured this swifty guy was just mentally ill and spouting a load of tosh, what memory once existed was gone at that time so she had no idea what swifty was trying to tell her about Jonny.

~ Tabitha knew somewhere deep down inside he was still that kind Jonny who taught her to ride a bike when she was four, even that was cut short when his mother screamed at him in the street to get in and he ran like the wind in fear jumping into the car. He did as he was told so much as a kid he rebelled to the limit once he was free from the apron strings. It's such a shame he went so far off the moral rails in life somewhere along the line. The way they live is such constant lies they have to live in an imaginary world and not slip up their real life to the made up one for the media. Do they live in big castles, half the time they hide away in small villages in an ordinary house and bribe the locals to keep their mouths shut, most people leave them alone.

It appears the ones closest to them are doing the harm but they don't see it. Did they make it up about Jonny and all them kids why bring it up during an attack? He wanted to brag about what he does for a living she thought but she wasn't interested in listening but it wasn't until years down the line it appeared the men were trying to harm women and friends of Jonny but why? To hurt him ? He can't afford to be mixing with these rum characters, heathen undesirables.

Let's hope he realsies, shoves them away before they damage him irreversibly.

Tabitha knows deep down Jonny has a good heart, he would never harm a child in any form because he knows what it's like to be on the receiving end of abuse. Nothing she can do but hope he is happy and if those kids are real and not rumors, hope they've been well looked after and please god he didn't introduce the men around him to them, heaven forbid. Does money bring nothing but weird mass breeding cults, secret families and love childs paid off to keep quiet.

Further more____.

It wasn't long before the rumors came round what exactly had happened in prison, the way he died wasn't what she had expected, they didn't drug him but they slowly tortured him and wanted him to feel every bit of pain also not be numbed in any form, they cut off his one remaining testile to start with, smashed in his knees, gouged out one of his eyes, they wanted him to watch the rest, sliced his body all over deep enough to sting but not kill him, death by a thousand cuts, in the end after breaking several bones they cut off his phallic manhood leaving him to bleed out during the night, they gagged him shoving a dirty sock in his mouth tied around tightly with a ripped bed sheet strip of material. Tied his arms tightly behind his back in the most uncomfortable position imaginable, partially dislocating his shoulder. He surely suffered, apparently the Ra and the cartel were arguing who was going to do it, eventually they came to a settlement joining forces but of course the guards didn't find any clues who it was. Perhaps it was too many in one place at one time and they all were each other's alibi.

Even if he did survive the fact they had stabbed him up the arse several times meant he'd be shitting in a bag for the rest of his life. ~Nobody mourned, nobody cared.

When you mix business with pleasure it's inevitable to see some of your staff being lower class peasants as he called them, they will inevitably turn and bite the hand that feeds them. Of course the number one rule was do not bite the hand that feeds you but he wasn't too bright in a social setting to see the hate behind his back. It was really sad to see someone who was once so sweet and kind and watch life and money twist him into a partial monster. Where did this little stig of the dump yeti funny guy go, scruffy bum looking man by day turn into a gangster by night involved in the dark side of social gatherings. Two personalities, or perhaps three. Nice, nasty and one that would swap heads every ten min from one to the other who you got you never know. It was perplexing to Tabitha how he had changed and damaged himself over the years.

She tried to hold onto the good memories and not think about the bad as life was coming along very well these days. Rumors had it the others involved in the child attacks had been paid a visit by gang members and pretty awful things happened to them, they were left with their mouths zipped in fear of retaliation they had got themselves in deep thinking money would be an easy way to buy having someone hurt and yet didn't realize once you are involved in that world they will keep coming back to you especially they know now they had money and ample amounts of it they'd be back for more it was a matter of time and possible blackmail ahead, and there's nowhere they can run to because no matter who is in that house whoever gets in their way will also be now involved in this big mess they started. The day came the women were raped infront of their husbands while they were tied up and forced to watch. All were beaten so badly, nobody was drugged, they wanted them to feel it all. They had to remember every bit of it. How else would they learn their lesson, what's the story? Did they think they can get away with raping a woman from a republican family are they stupid there is no wrath worse than them related to the IRA. Part of the reason it was taken on was because it was English men harming Irish families. The rest was personal. __He's not finished yet!

Luke was a Irishman Tabitha had met through the family he was deeply involved in politics, over the years she would hear of orders being given discussing the facts she would over hear the men in the family discussing things she didn't fully understand, it was so hush hush and she wasn't supposed to hear, and showed out the room when she was caught earwigging. There was a strong discrimination of Irish to English, even Jonny wasn't welcome in the gate, he was keen on Tabitha they were friends they had this sneak off meet and go boating having fun growing up all before he changed and got into the movies more deeply he wasn't the same man any more. She remembers his mum shouting at him, swiping for his head to make him sit back down at the piano to play and practice, when he was a teen. He was molded into who he is. He had now become bitter and moody like someone had broken his heart so deeply he would never love again she felt looking inward to how he talked. He would often run out Tabitha's gate as a fist was waved. "Get out you limey heathen, go away wit u !"___ the anger in her grandfather's voice he would have taken an ax to his head if he had stood around long enough. Tabitha's grandparents hated him they knew and heard of what he had become with women from his grandmother who was saying she hoped he would stop the galavanting and just settle down with one but he couldn't stay loyal this to an older generation wasn't something they could see fit in any form to excepting. It was a shame they were right in hindsight.

But his good side was slightly more than his bad, it's down to him to work on himself. One day he will grow up or learn the hard way. When the family had to do their jobs, politics they called it, there would be Irish rebel songs blaring on the gramophone to cover what was being discussed. They made no English friends and

Tabitha wasn't allowed to either but she was a rebel and went out and did what she liked..the constant nagging of the ear when she got home. Why are they mixing with the likes of them? It was exhausting to say the least she upped left home as a teen and that was all linked to Jonny he had her evicted because they were caught on the village hall getting it on when they had been partying one day, and for that being his fault in the first place but all his instigating he had her kicked out the village so she was made homeless they threatened to kick her out on the streets or the grandparents had to go too, and for them to keep their house which was under the control of Jonny as he had shares in the houses in the area nad part of the round table group she just went.

This didn't stop him visiting her when she moved into every house she ever lived in he would visit at some point down the line. H couldn't stay away.

It wasn't healthy.

He had a love hate thing going on in his head.

CHAPTER FOUR

It was at this point when the memories of the bad things Jonny had done were now surfacing, she would tell him no if she didn't agree to his orders but he didn't like to be told no. He called himself a pimp sometimes she would tell him "stop acting like a prick," but he would treat women badly in-front of her and she couldn't make him listen to reason, this angered him as he's stubborn, when refused he would get so angry and have the girls chucked out of the clubs and guess who that was; swiftly one of the men who he would promise women to against their will. 'Vile'. Swifty was spiking the women who went back to Jonny's place so they wouldn't remember where he lived and unveiled who he was. That isn't ok, they had an illegal sex act going down.

When they were young; She was stronger than him anyway; they'd had many fights, him punching her in the leg was this thing and she'd kick him in the balls for it. Then he ran off upset. Her leg would be black and blue the next day, but it wasn't like a real fight. It was more of them two used to give each other a wallop when the other was driving, a dead leg a dead arm. They thought it was funny in their youth before kids came alone. This is why each pregnancy she had and of all of them there was always a small chance one of the children may be his but she didn't test them all she kept her mouth shut.

All Tabitha was solely interested in was having the people involved who hurt her kids dealt with once and for all and to make sure they can no longer get near kids again. Jonny's grandmother was right about him all along and her fear for him destroying himself was looking like you take so much power into your hands and you self explode. That's him now.

When Tabitha was having the abortion Jonny was screaming murderer and begged her to keep it offering one hundred grand to keep it, it was during the years of memory loss. The thing is it was a consideration that

Jonny, who was the one who taught swifty taking him under his wing into the perverted sexual lifestyle at an early stage, teaching him it's ok to drive underage on the roads breaking the law to sneak about behind his wife's back.

He couldn't use his normal drivers or taxi as they'd find out where he lived but now swiftly has a hold over Jonny holding all his darkest secrets. Only problem is swifty was going out into bars and bragging to everyone how he does it all telling everyone Jonny's sexual stories.

He was making money talking to the papers. How could Jonny not see right under his nose the only person who knows about all his kids are his personal staff. He must be high on drugs to not see what was happening as his empire was at risk of being brought to rubble.

Swifty was drugging the women and bringing them back to the mansion blindfolded and taken home before they woke they would remember nothing the next day. The ogre wants to bring him down with him perhaps? Why is he saying all this about Jonny?

By this point it was apparent that some of the dark memories were still suppressed, but she felt a stage of anger raising.

She knew him as kind but something wasn't there, no spark just a close friend who she had a good laugh with that was as far as her feelings went, perhaps she wasn't capable of love. Tabitha was a teen for god's sake she wasn't ready for sex yet he made that happen her first time was meant to be special not a one nt stand. You can't suddenly look at a man you have known all your life as a friend and suddenly find him attractive. It wasn't so much looks more what she'd seen him do to other women that put her breaks on. It doesn't work that way and she couldn't bring herself to think of him that way. She never slept with Jonny sober for a reason, she would need to be in a frame of mind to not feel shy, even though she had a good body, perfect body in fact not a flaw on it, she was young and shy she was raised different to him he was the total opposite. He was too open minded, the way of life he chose to take. How could she have been so close to him and seen the kindness in him for so many years and yet see he had two sides, one sadistic and cruel, the other kind the boy he used to be growing up.

What happened to him to make him so messed up? She recalls visiting him when he had girlfriends she would pop in and they all looked like they were tranquilized and slurring words almost. But why was swifty so mad at him? What did he do to Swifty to make him hate him so much? All these questions I'm sure will be answered as time goes by. At this stage the past was flying in on a roll. The question is what should Tabitha do with this knowledge, and how many others are in the same boat. Elan had tried to warn Tabitha they had sat for hours talking when he reached over and held her hand, by this point she was nervous and also tired. She wanted to go home, she was wondering if he was the same way, but he sparked up another conversation. He tried to say his friends are into mass breeding and he disagreed, but at the time she wasn't sure who he meant then the penny dropped. Elan seemed keen on Tabitha. They had talked all day going onto that evening, she wore herself out there wasn't anything left to talk about. She wanted to go home to bed. She kinda liked him but it really was the wrong place at the wrong time.

If they had met a few years before or a year after who knows perhaps she'd let him change her world like he said he would.

In hindsight she thought he was nice actually and his honesty was a refreshing change to the usual men she had met. She soon realized the propaganda was all fake but she knew the affairs were real.

There was a time Tabitha's boyfriends would be telling Jonny to stay away from my girlfriend, he would come over to say hi in bars when she was out on a date. It practically ruined every date he would just ruin it. Like clear off now what did you say to wreck that for her she couldn't get a man let alone keep one in the end. This was the 90s.

Years on; He got so mad one time he blurted out about her being in the movie and how he had done so much for her and she didn't appreciate it.

She had amnesia you twat ! What part of amnesia do you not understand ? ...he was trying to spark her memory, yet he couldn't understand why she didn't ever recognise him. This frustrated him and could hold it for about twenty mins and then explode.

CHAPTER FIVE

They say all the truth comes out in the end so let's just try and get back on the tracks of why there is some good that comes from all this. But they do say people of less intelligence are more honest. Although no, take that back, there's no way a pervert is honest.

There's no point in trying to analyze someone else when what needs to be focused on is the actual criminal himself and how did Jonny get mixed up with him or involved in his life he would have known he was a pervert from the news he would have known from the orgy's he helped him organize at the mansion. But why did he keep him around so closely ? He must have something on him to blackmail him with he must have ammo. It's a process of elimination one step at a time and Tabitha was determined to get to the bottom of it no matter what the cost. {They say when someone is telling a story and it makes their own life worse, it's usually the truth.}

At this stage she was feeling like the woman next door to Jeffrey Dalhmer when she kept telling the police what she was suspicious of yet nobody listened. That's very similar except the police were listening. She was determined to get justice for the children no matter what even if it means.

The attackers; No stone will go unturned where she is concerned. It's her turn to mess with their heads now and draw them out into the open. Why hadn't the police taken all their devices and checked for child porn she knew they had because Swifty was stupid enough to tell her that during the attack, one of many slip of the tongues he loosely told her as he believed she wouldn't ever remember it. The police by this stage have enough details all the stones unturned and being unturned gathering their evidence to bring down the other guilty parties, they have to of panicked by now and disposed of all their photos and hard drives, but old social media accounts they used to share dark images will still be able to be found. Old phone numbers can be looked into. They will be handed a sentence to the full extent of the law if it's the last thing that is done once and for all, unless the gangs get to them first.

Tabitha is the one of the worst enemies to have as money means nothing to her it doesn't control her or bribe her, there will be no pay off hush money here they will try but it will be in vain. She's more head strong than the average girl next door who crumbles at the thought of a fight, she's the type to see two men fighting and run and jump on one their backs and shove her fingers in his eyes and gouge them out to help the other.

Tabitha would have days out and bump into Jonny for the last five years. She would pretend to not see him or know him now. She couldn't be bothered with it or explaining by this point, she had let it all go and didn't see the point in ever telling him she remembers him now, as their lives were so separate and neither of them were the two youngsters who knew each other back to front no longer. They no longer exist; the people they were before have gone for good. He was still saying Hi like he always did she drinks in one of his bars sometimes but felt no obligation to talk now he's gone the person who she knew, his personality is gone his looks are even different trying too hard to stay young died black hair still long and scruffy sweaty overly layered clothes sometimes he tried to dress normal and it wasn't him who was he even now? He became ordinary. Something reached in and took his personality with it, the warmth was gone, something had hurt him and he had changed.

While she was processing all this she didn't want to complicate and have him bring in a hostile defense to his pervert friend even Jonny couldn't change her mind at this point, she was out for the kill for the lot of them (methodically speaking).

He worked for a paper when he wasn't working for the film industry so he had power over what was printed and having a mate in radio he had power over spreading idle gossip she was told by one of his staff. He would use it to write his own press and take his own photos and he would stage them to look like the press caught him but this made Tabitha laugh as sometimes the photos in the paper she was there when they were taken so she knew who took them and the exact spot it was taken.

She kept shhh tho took a step back and left him to it she could see how the media worked and realized it wasn't all it's cut out to be and it certainly wasn't a honest place to be. The photos stated he was in France or America but he was here in a hometown. The background blurred but she was standing behind the photographer so she knew but still …. Hush hush she was very good at keeping a secret for him. He would make her promise to "please don't tell anyone about us"!, don't tell anyone, it's really important, so she kept all his secrets out of loyalty until her memory was gone but loyalty didn't exist any more he was a stranger again that's what she manifested it to be anyway perhaps her brain shut him out for a reason.

CHAPTER SIX

Jonny always had a joint hanging out his mouth. His hair was messy, he wore a ton of foundation on tv and make-up eyeliner the lot as they do. She has a scar on her breast when he was mad once he put a joint out on her breast and ran off. She was heavily pregnant at the time with her first child and he felt he had the right to argue over her cravings for black pudding, that's how silly it got. They would laugh all day and suddenly he'd flip for no reason but it was a silly pathetic tantrum and he'd run off. He was a harmless bag of wind when it came to a fight it was her who really had the temper. He didn't stick around, he showed a clean pair of heels before things got that heated. But they'd calm down the next day and forget all about the petty rows.

__Tabitha had no choice at this stage but to obey and hand over all she knew about those involved. Who ended up dead at this stage felt like it was on her but she didn't want to be intertwined in this dark place. The IRA and the cartel weren't happy about working together but it brain a brotherhood nevertheless, it was shocking how they bonded bantered about women and liqueur smokes and motors, who knew the hells angels were so involved in this too, until a load of them pulled up asking who Bia and her family was they wanted to know every detail and they demanded it all. They weren't stupid they knew when Bia had lied they knew her family had lied they knew they were to put this record straight in the end.

Were they aware one of the old men who did the rape made up a profligate story all along and somehow the others was in on the lies were they paid or were they just trying to clear the fellas sick name. The court decided the physical damages outweighed the story the men came up with the fact that nine months later the dna proved one of the men was the father of her child a rape child. Not only had she subjected to this gruesome rape gruesome disrespect from Jonny because he wanted a story for his local paper how would he of liked his home address and personal issues to be exposed. A journalist was arrested and a policeman was suspended due to getting the investigation gravely wrong which led to them not getting a long enough sentence, consequently they did serve some time in prison as the jury saw through their fictional pleas.

None of the evidence added up to their story being true but the injuries were so far beyond repair that it was a life changing error via the hands of the law.

Tabitha's mind drifted back yet again to that repeating summer's day memory where she always walked along the river banks. There was somewhere to go, something to do, there wasn't much else there to do in the village; it was so far in the middle of nowhere. She got as far as the field by the river when she was met by Jonny, he was with a friend, he had a strange look upon his face pleased to see her but something was off with his behavior, she wasn't sure what it was as she was a naive girl then, she smiled back and tried to pass him by but he was blocking her path every way she went to go in this big field and his friend she shouted no Jonny leave her alone just stop, like she knew he was just determined to chat to her, it was like a challenge to him. She finally got past him by giving him a look of get out my fuck-in way, she maybe small but she knew how to look after herself if it came to a scrap she had a mighty temper and maybe wouldn't win against a man but sure would leave a few marks, she was known to bite off body parts in scraps which got her a bad name.

It was then he turned heels and went back to the river bank where she was just walking to sit down and paddle her toes in to cool off. The summer was always great there by the weir where you could swim for free in a beauty spot. Shame he was there she thought for some reason that day he was just annoying her, she thinks he's drunk as he wasn't acting himself at all. He jumped in the river and climbed onto the tractor inner-tube he had persuaded the local farm laborer to give him that morning as she saw him there begging like a tool. Why beg, go and buy one if you have money, she thought.

She'd been sitting there fifteen minutes or so watching him jumping in and out of the water being facetious in front of everybody. It was wearing thin. She was about to get up and go home as swimming with him there probably meant he might try and do something silly so she figured it's safer to leave. At that point he came over sat by her on the bank and handed her a beer, she wasn't a drinker and hadn't had beer at that stage, much, so it went right to her head, to a point she had woken up the next day at 10:30am the other side of the field with her bra and top lifted up and her underwear gone. She vaguely remembers talking to him on the bank and was laying down in the dark in the corner of the field because she wasnt able to get up, he said leaning over her, i'm going to teach you a lesson and removed her clothing, pulled apart her legs and the next thing the words fuck it came from his mouth as he climbed onto her she could tell he was carerssing her body but she just went to sleep it wasn't something she could stay awake for it over powered her the beer he had given her.

By time she woke up and she was alone the next day dressed herself as he had flung her clothes atray. She went home feeling dizzy and unwell. She went back to bed and back to work the next day as usual and had put it behind her that she had lost her virginity in such an awful way as she wasn't fully conscious and two she wanted it to be with someone she was in a relationship with not a wham bam thank you man. Which to him was all he knew how to do. She never thought anything about it until her period hadn't arrived, she knew she was pregnant already but started to see someone else and hid it well, so by time she worked out he was pregnant it was a panic and wasn't sure how far gone she was, she led her boyfriend to think it was his but after seeing the dr she it was six weeks before she even met him.

She was in the bar one evening the night before the abortion, Jonny came sat by her and whispered Teresa are you pregnant? Yes I'm going tomorrow morning to get rid though, he whispered back. "If you want to keep it I can help you if you like. I feel responsible." "No I can't. I'm too young my family would go mad and kick me out on the streets and I'd lose it anyways," "no, Teresa raises his voice in concern. "I can help you keep it. I'd like you to keep it. "She made it clear that the lad she was now with couldn't find out about them. But Jonny walked up to him and tried to talk him into letting her keep the baby to which he piped up in a vile aggressive temper towards Jonny like he knew the baby was his," no that baby has to die tomorrow." She overheard him shout and stay away from my girlfriend. Jonny ran out and left the pub.

She soon realized he wasn't for her he was quite a spiteful person and went ahead with the abortion but left that lad too he had forced her into a choice she didn't have time to choose herself, she felt like she could feel it moving round in her womb she knew she was much further gone her belly was hard and grown already, it had to be birth as she was too far gone. It was done now and she was too young and immature anyway in reality she would have failed being a good mother so young she needed to wait and grow up and settle down before she did that. Life experiences she needed and she had it all come in the end if life was wisdom she was top of it by time she had reached her fifties.

Over the years she had two abortions of Johnny's one night stand antics with her and she miscarried one. Just when she thought she had it all, another memory would roll in. They were still flooding in here and there but mostly good memories now she didn't feel the need to connect back with anyone from the past at this point. She had no desire to ever tell him about the baby loss after the hospital. Early on when it was all being pieced together she wanted him to help her fill in the missing pieces but they eventually came back by themselves. Thanks to the people who lied to her when she asked for truthful memories she was able to see through the liars, it gave her a fly on the wall experience because she already knew the truth at this stage.

She kept running into him in local bars, but she played the game pretending she didn't notice him when she saw him in the Hotel, there was no need to reach out for help any longer she had figured it all out alone. Why did he choose to stay in the one she was posted to? Why does fate keep placing them in the same bloody places? It's Mid summer and a heatwave which she hates. She was sorting through the linen room when he came running along the corridor and tried to open the fire escape saying it's hot. She caught him sneaking into the linen room as well taking sheets and towels, what is he like ? It was like 'go away' at this point she had enough of her memories she didn't want to see anymore of him. She had reached the point in which she was just avoiding facing him, he always says hi still today but she still isn't ready to talk. She's finally at a place of closure, with him anyway.

CHAPTER SEVEN

Reflecting back, was that the source of all her troubles all along the beginning of her womanhood taken by Jonny who just wanted to use her for sex and no feelings at all? She became molded into this hard woman who's heart could no longer be reached, over the years she learned to use him the same way he used her. Subsequently, then forthcoming, nothing could break down that wall of brick she built up around herself in the course of time, hence concluding from that period onward nothing and nobody would be able to touch her heart ever again.

There was seven people left to meet their karma, this meant seven more crimes predicted a stratagem of planning their fate that would equally match the stories they had manifested themselves to justify their crimes and their lies told. There was no way of letting this go, as much as she would tell herself to it was a burning anger within she had to cross the line to avenge what they did to her kids, so in her wrath she will carefully plan her next move even if it means their demise then so be it. She could foresee them suffering immense pain, she would need to evolve into the person she didn't want to be. The justice system was very poor at helping women, children, victims of rape and abuse, it was very male orientated, they leaned toward helping getting men off, the courts were definitely in favour of men. There was a plan; the mind of the woman who planned it needed to be tamed, the big man's body parts and his desires were removed, now it was her turn to suffer so that she can no longer harm children from there on, cured of her mental illness once and for all, taken out. This was the only cure, other than ending up behind bars Bia was a drug addict alcoholic who would at some point revert back to her old ways under pressure, and boy she was about to see pressure, Tabitha would pilot the course forward that would make sure she would suffer for hurting her children Bia had used her mental illness to get away with so much, used it to justify all her crimes that it was by this stage wearing very thin, how she kept getting away with lying to the law, patience was thin on the ground and Tabitha had to keep control of her old temper if she were to bump into her. No witnesses could see her when she saw [red out] which Tabitha would experience during fights. It takes a lot to lose her temper. She's unperturbed until someone hurts her family then it's __'get out the way,' clear the path!

There was a desolation having to fight this all alone, there were people trying to stop her along with some others' perspective of revenge and their own thoughts on wrath, a 'pique'!

There was now a list; a list of those named, a list of places they lived and a list of bars they visited including a list of all the alleyways and roads home at night. Would it be a night time though or would it be an equal random day time war break out that would be made to look like an accident. This was beginning to feel sinister but it had to come to such a brutal end. Her mind had gone from no leave it no it's not worth it but as time went by she felt herself being drawn to this life she hadn't wanted to be involved in all along, ~ the republican blood in her was about to rise to the surface, don't mess with girl who's blood runs rich with Irish dna, her upbringing and who she knew she had the power in her hands but she wanted this to be her fight and her alone. She had allowed them to deal with the giant fat pig of a man but she didn't like to call him a man, but a monster. They had that desire and due to his size she let them. On the other hand, ~ the women were now hers.

One night she was out and it was just pure luck she stumbled upon one of the women who were tipsy on their way home, Tabtiha felt the need at high speed to follow behind just to scare her she wanted her to know she was there she would make a point of shouting abuse at her," keep ya eyes peeled I'm coming for ya very soon bitch", this sparked the girl up to pulling out her phone so Tabitha would act natural and make her look paranoid at this stage but she knew the mental torture she'd do this until the last days on earth and make the rest of their lives hell. Tabitha was at this point untrammeled due to being the sort of woman usually keeping an impassive face to danger, by this point she was used to it. She wanted to test the waters of course she would only attack on surprise there would be no time to pull out the phone when the time comes for real but she wanted them to know they were on the list. Per contra howbeit she feels the more uncomfortable she could make their lives the better, however long it takes.

A year went by and she had almost forgotten about her fury. She felt her life had moved on, she was happy in a great place, money was rolling in, she had purchased a home, she had moved to her dream country, and met and finally settled down with a good man. It took her till her old age, she was now in her sixties close to retirement, her body was old she ached most of the time but happy and content. She had't thought about revenge for about ten years or so deciding prison wasn'tworth the bother, two of them had died of natural causes this was music to her ears they had died, she found the need to buy a bottle of bubbly when she heard of their passing due to their part in planning the rapes of her small children and taking part in some of the spiking by their own hands involved, all them years ago, so as cruel as it sounds its a natural thing to feel many would of by now killed the person who harmed their kids.

Many would be doing time for revenge and the thoughts were certainly there bubbling under the surface hoping she didn't stumble on a opportunity to smack one of them in the face with whatever she could grab at hand the thoughts were there she would see "red out" and all hell would break loose that inner temper she had as a teenager was deeply buried and it frightened her she didn't want to risk it now. She visited the graves and made sure that Bia knew she had visited, she would casually leave a orange juice carton on top of the headstones, this would play havoc with Bias psychosis, the tables had turned she was playing mind games wanting her to gain the knowledge sparking the paranoia, tormenting her to a place of instability so she would need to up her medication. This would bring joy to Tabitha knowing it was ticking her over the edge. All Tabitha could think of during moments like this would be ~ karma has arrived.

It wasn't so much incredibly careful planning but fortunate that fate seemed to be sorting itself. She was skeptical but oddly things kept falling into place, the murder would be momentous in her mind but the inner self control of her isn't worth prison she isn't worth prison let her be her own actions of who she was during her life will catch up to her and them all by itself. All Tabitha had to do was listen closely and celebrate when she heard bad news had touched their lives in one way or another. Inconclusively therefore it was apparent at this time of life she had found some peace but a little desire laid deep to overhaulthe distribution of torment the aforementioned was still laying deep beneath.

CHAPTER EIGHT

Tabitha had gone over this memory many times before it kept popping up as a result of revisiting the house she'd be there and it would force a flashback every time of the murder of her nan. The day she went to visit her nan she made a mistake of taking an unstable Bia with her extreme psychosis she had no idea how bad she had reached with her illness. It feels like going over old ground but let's relive it once more; Tabitha was in the kitchen while Bia was sitting talking to nan in the living room. The nan had said I'm telling the police what you did. I know what you did. Suddenly Bia launches up from the sofa and attacks the old lady, Tabitha see's this from the other room and runs in and grabs Bia off her like a rag doll. What are you doing? She was fuming so she hoofed her out the door and took her back to her hometown just a few miles down the road.

She then drove home but had an odd feeling and went back to the house about 45 min to a hr later. There was sitting Bia and Tabitha's nan still in her chair but this time next to her was cartons of orange juice. She raised one up with her right hand and sounded drunk. Her eyes looked funny and her hair was all messed up; it looked like it was being pulled and she'd been attacked. Bia was clearly high on drugs by this time and acting odd trying to pretend to be innocent. She said Bia said sorry, she brought me some orange juices raising one up like a toast, but her mouth dropped like she was having a stroke or she lost all muscle ability. As she peeked in the back kitchen her gramp and mother were asleep, orange juices [unbeknown till years to come these were laced by Bia] on the table next to them they were drugged. This was out of character; they never sleep in the day. But Tabitha had no idea or she'd of rang the police and she'd of beaten Bia half to death with her bare hands or worse took her life her temper was red, and she had no control if she lost it. She grabbed Bia up by the shoulders and hoofed her back in the car and took her home as she was clearly on drugs, she asked then demanded do not go visit my family again ok, you are not welcome there you disrespected my nan today, you attacked her I mean it stay away or i'll kill ya. The next day Tabitha was woken by her mum ringing around -7:30 am," Nanny's dead!" She sat up in shock but her mother was unable to tell her any more. [Her mother had a low IQ so she wasn't able to express herself like a normal person.]

Tabitha was down in the village dealing with the funeral and the family standing outside the house when she received a call from her nans dr. "hello Tabitha I had no other way of calling as your family don't have a phone, but the autopsy results said she had some unusual drug in her system, now I'm aware she was in a great deal of pain with gout and it's nothing to do with me but this could either spark a murder investigation or left perhaps she took it for pain and I think we can go with that." Tabitha, concerned by this, asked what was the drug she had in her system but he refused to tell her then cut the call short this left her confused. She was none the wiser but he did say she had heart failure and that drug probably didn't help.

Now the day of the funeral all the family were standing outside the house Bia had called and asked Tabitha when it was and good luck with it, she had still not got any suspicions to anything untoward had happened at this point. So on the day a big man turned up and handed out loads of free orange juice to everyone, nobody wanted one except Sean, he took the lot he was thirsty, the others didn't want it. So everyone was around the grave and suddenly Tabitha's turn to throw in a handful of dirt after the coffin was lowered and this weird mentally ill man jumped out of nowhere and angrily shoved Tabitha into the grave. Sean walked across the cemetery and pulled her up while the odd drunk man was falling all over the place shouting and swearing that's from Bia "she killed her, and she wants you dead next."

Sean was fuming not at my nans funeral you fucker, come on lads, he grabs the man by the scruff of the neck in a vile temper and all the men group to take him behind a wall and kick his head in, you hear a scream and the next time tabitha see him his arm was in plaster they broken his arm. Shame it wasn't his neck. One of her aunts had said to her months later, if gramp dies it's your fault if it wasn't for you taking that woman down there nan would still be alive. Tabitha didn't understand any of this; she only figured she was stemming her anger at her because the aunt was always a mean old bitch since she was a kid, a spiteful wicked one of them all. If she had had all this epiphany come memories sooner this would have all been dealt with permanently hitherto. What is she supposed to do with it all these years later? As a result,__ one evening Bia had gotten immensely drunk as always and confessed to the murder of the grandmother giving her story confessing it all to Tabitha, she begged her for her forgiveness but then went on to having her kids attacked not long after so her mental illness was never going to be cured or forgiven. ~ She can burn in hell.

At that time Tabitha hadn't even begun to regain her memories so what Bia was telling her unbeknown to Bia was her own death sentence.

Concequently_____.

_The unapprehended were all directly under the radar of the CID.

___With a 'Retribution' impending!

_____Who will get to them first ?

SYNOPSIS

This Unique Book 'The Agnostic' has been written by the Author Mia Collins as a final 'fictional' episode to Sangfroid and How Do You Know My Name. The story awakens poignant memories for Tabitha, she was never very cathartic so this was extraordinarily unusual. With an added twist of 'fictional character' names to give the feel of power to their stature. It includes an extended file of unsolved crime patterns that were left hanging by the CID. Psychopaths live among us. Never take safety for granted. Amidst this story it provides an in depth sequel of events that lead to the enlightenment of a string of major crimes and criminals tricks of the trade to how they get away with their felonious acts who thrive on flagrant narcissism, but once they've taken that vicious lane there's no turning back from the world of malefactors who were now honed on retribution.

Please check out; 'Sangfroid and How Do You Know My Name' as the first two books in this unique three part short series. Therefore will enlighten a more lucid portrayal of this poignant story.

Milton Keynes UK
Ingram Content Group UK Ltd.
UKHW010621250624
444673UK00001B/27

9 781669 890737